WIDGET

Lyn Rossiter McFarland   Pictures by Jim McFarland

SQUARE FISH • Farrar Straus Giroux • New York

To Abbie, Muffin, and Widget

SQUARE
FISH
An Imprint of Macmillan

Square Fish and the Square Fish logo are trademarks of Macmillan and
are used by Farrar Straus Giroux under license from Macmillan.

Library of Congress Cataloging-in-Publication Data
McFarland, Lyn Rossiter.
Widget / Lyn Rossiter McFarland ; pictures by Jim McFarland.
p.   cm.
Summary: A small stray dog is accepted into a household full of cats by learning to "fit in,"
but when his mistress is hurt, he demonstrates that being a dog is not all bad.
ISBN 978-0-374-48386-9
[1. Dogs—Fiction. 2. Cats—Fiction.] I. McFarland, Jim, 1935–ill. II. Title.
PZ7.M4784614 Wi 2001   [E]—dc21   00-62274

Originally published in the United States by Farrar Straus Giroux
First Square Fish Edition: August 2012
Square Fish logo designed by Filomena Tuosto
mackids.com

23 25 27 29 30 28 26 24

AR: 1.5 / F&P: J / LEXILE: BR

Widget was a little stray dog.
He had no home.
He had no friends.

He was very sad and lonely.
He was cold and hungry, too.

He saw a house at the end of a road.
There was a door just his size. He peeked inside.

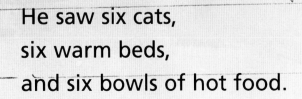

He saw six cats,
six warm beds,
and six bowls of hot food.

Widget dove for the food—
and straight into Mrs. Diggs!

"Why, you poor thing," said Mrs. Diggs.
"I wish you could stay. But I'm afraid the girls just
 can't stand dogs."

Widget looked at the girls.
He looked at Mrs. Diggs.
She seemed so nice.
Widget really wanted
   to stay.

"Meow?" said Widget.

Mrs. Diggs laughed.

"Well, girls," she said. "What do you think?"

The girls puffed up.

Widget puffed up.

The girls hissed and spit.

Widget hissed and spit.

The girls growled.

Widget purred . . . played with a toy mouse . . .
and used the litter box.

The girls stopped growling.
They were confused.
Widget looked like a dog. He smelled like a dog.
But he acted like a cat!

Mrs. Diggs set a bowl down for Widget.
Widget started eating.
He never took his eyes off the girls.

The girls started eating.

They never took their eyes off Widget.

"Why, you fit right in," said Mrs. Diggs to Widget.

And Widget did fit right in.
From that day on, Widget ran with the girls,
played with the girls, and curled up with the girls.

In fact, he had so much fun
with the girls he sometimes
forgot he was a dog!

One day, Mrs. Diggs tripped on a toy and fell down.
She didn't move.
Widget and the girls were worried.

They meowed for help.
No one came.

They screeched. They yowled.
They caterwauled for help.
No one came.

Then Widget barked for help.
The girls were shocked!

Then they barked for help, too.

Everyone came.
Mrs. Diggs was saved!

"I didn't know you had a dog," said a neighbor.

"Oh, yes," said Mrs. Diggs.

"It's nice to have a dog. Right, girls?"

Oh, yes, the girls agreed.